Saliman
AND THE
Memory
Stone

BY ERICA LYONS
ILLUSTRATED BY YINON PTAHIA

APPLES & HONEY PRESS

To my sons Yitzhak and Itai — E.L.

To my grandparents and Aunt Rachel who also made their way from Yemen to Israel — Y.P.

A note from the artist: To create the contours of Yemen from more than a century ago, I used a textured ink brush to make designs that resemble the brush strokes from traditional Yemenite books and scrolls. For the color, I used a grunge brush to make the illustrations look like an old painting that had faded a bit with time. The main colors are red and brown, taking us back to the high red mountains of Yemen, and to the colorful fabrics, clothing, and jewelry of Yemen.

With gratitude for the expert guidance of Menashe Anzi, senior lecturer in the department of Jewish History at Ben-Gurion University, with a focus on the Jews of Yemen and the Indian Ocean.

Apples & Honey Press
An Imprint of Behrman House Publishers
Millburn, New Jersey 07041
www.applesandhoneypress.com

ISBN 978-1-68115-631-6

Text copyright © 2024 by Erica Lyons
Illustrations copyright © 2024 by Behrman House

Library of Congress Cataloging-in-Publication Data

Names: Lyons, Erica, author. | Ptahia, Yinon, illustrator.
Title: Saliman and the memory stone / by Erica Lyons ; illustrated by Yinon Ptahia.
Description: Millburn, New Jersey : Apples & Honey Press, 2024. | Audience: Ages 3-6. | Audience: Grades K-1. | Summary: In 1881 Yemen, six-year-old Saliman holds his memory stone tight to remind him of home as he and his family journey on foot to Jerusalem.
Identifiers: LCCN 2023037176 | ISBN 9781681156316 (hardcover)
Subjects: CYAC: Jews--Fiction. | Voyages and travels--Fiction. | Memory--Fiction. | Yemen (Republic)--Fiction. | Jerusalem--Fiction. | LCGFT: Picture books.
Classification: LCC PZ7.1.L965 Sal 2024 | DDC [E]--dc23
LC record available at https://lccn.loc.gov/2023037176

Design and art direction by Zach Marell
Edited by Dena Neusner
Printed in China

9 8 7 6 5 4 3 2 1

0924/B2628/A6

Saliman was born
when the moon was full and round
and the rains refused to come.

Sukkot, the harvest festival,
had come and gone six times
when Saliman's family began
their journey from a village
outside Sana'a in Yemen.

The warm fall winds blew
as his sisters stacked pita high
in baskets they had woven.
His *um* gathered blankets,
hiding silver jewelry and their holy
Torah in between.

His *ab* sold their goats
in a nearby village and Saliman cried,
but not before lifting their soft ears to
whisper a promise
that he would remember
their names and the color of their fur.

"They're not ours to keep,
the goats or the land.
Yemen is a borrowed place,"
his *jad* said.

"Our home is far across the sands and seas in Jerusalem. There we will have a life of plenty, among our people. It was written in the Song of Songs that the time to return is now."

So Saliman tried to memorize
the smell of meat roasting and fresh ground chili,
the shape of the mountains,
and the pattern the moon made when it crept
through the windowpanes.
He slipped a loose stone from the base of his house
into his pocket.
He called it his memory stone.

When the sun rose the next day, they all set out
in a great caravan along with their neighbors,
more than twenty families in total.
Donkeys carried their burdens.

Young and old they walked and walked.
Sandstorms blew and erased
even Yemen's jagged mountains.
Um covered Saliman's eyes and mouth
with her scarf.

Some days there was no water to drink
and the air was so dry
Saliman thought he would crack like the earth.
Still they walked.

Sleeping under the stars
as his ancestors in the Torah did long ago,
Saliman held his stone to his cheek.

When it was hot out, the stone was cool
like the tiles of his bedroom,
and in his dreams he was back there again

Some nights, with his stone in his hands,
Saliman sat with the men.
Ab danced and Jad recited poetry.

From the other side of the camp
Um's beautiful voice rose above
the other women's.

Back in the village,
they had danced to their ancestral tunes.
Silver jewelry jingled under the starry skies.

Now, under the hot sun, Saliman and
his sisters tried to walk to those beats.
They were songs of memory.
He held his stone close to his heart.

Weeks became months,
months of walking and walking.
Saliman was tired and hungry.

Some days Um
divided a single
piece of pita
among all of them.
Some days there
was none.

Many people became ill.
Saliman's family had to
sell their donkeys and
soon their silver, too,
for passage on a ship
that would take them
only partway.

"We have nothing left," Saliman cried out.
"We have our songs and our stories piled
high on our backs," Ab said.

That night, under the stars on the rough sea, Saliman traced the deep wrinkles on Jad's palm.

"They're a map so we'll remember where we've been," said Jad.

Like their ancestors
who had wandered the desert long ago,
the large caravan passed through Egypt too,
moving from port to port by ship and on foot.
Their melodies followed them.

Outside his tent, Saliman drew pictures
with his stone of the goats he had left behind.
And he began to understand.
Yemen was a part of him no matter where
he traveled.

When they finally arrived in Jaffa on another ship,
they were close, but still not there yet,
so they walked some more.
They slept in dark caves,
and with his stone, Saliman etched a picture
of his old village, in the earth.

"Soon we will build a beautiful new house,"
Ab said.
"But we're barefoot and empty bellied,"
Saliman's sister cried.
"We have everything we need in our hearts,"
Ab reminded her.

One day when the sky was the color of the sea, a glimmering golden city stretched out before them.
The Tower of David, from the Song of Songs, glistened.
They had finally reached Jerusalem.

When the gates to the city opened,
Saliman entered with Yemenite tunes on his lips
and his stone, the color of his old house
in the village, in his hand.

Memory had followed him
from afar.

Saliman's humming filled the narrow alleyways.

Soon the others joined in too.

Their stories danced inside the open-air market.

Their poems sounded through the stalls.

And when Sukkot, the harvest
festival, began again,
Saliman's family celebrated just
as they had before,

making new memories
and dreaming of old
ones too.

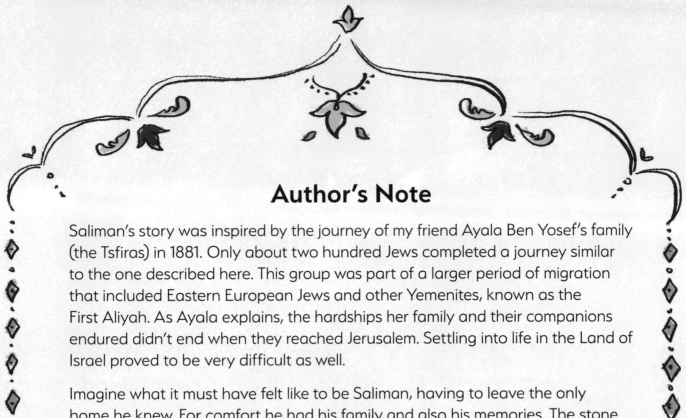

Author's Note

Saliman's story was inspired by the journey of my friend Ayala Ben Yosef's family (the Tsfiras) in 1881. Only about two hundred Jews completed a journey similar to the one described here. This group was part of a larger period of migration that included Eastern European Jews and other Yemenites, known as the First Aliyah. As Ayala explains, the hardships her family and their companions endured didn't end when they reached Jerusalem. Settling into life in the Land of Israel proved to be very difficult as well.

Imagine what it must have felt like to be Saliman, having to leave the only home he knew. For comfort he had his family and also his memories. The stone he carried also helped him to remember what Yemen was like. Do you have a special object that reminds you of home?

While other Jews also emigrated from Yemen in the years following the First Aliyah, the largest emigration of Yemenite Jews occurred much later, in 1949, after the establishment of the modern State of Israel. In that year, nearly forty-five thousand Yemenite Jews were transported by plane to Israel in response to increasing persecution and political changes in Yemen, coupled with their desire to return to the land of their ancestors. Only a few Jews remain in Yemen today.

Where does your family live? Where did they or their parents or grandparents come from originally? Did they speak a different language from you? Did they bring any special foods or songs or objects with them? Talk to your parents or an older relative to learn more about your family's journey.

Words to Know

Ab: father

Jad: grandfather

Song of Songs: a love poem in the Bible, also called the Song of Solomon

Sukkot: a Jewish harvest festival in which people build huts to represent the journey of the ancient Israelites

Torah: the first five books of the Hebrew Bible

Um: mother

Ayala's Kubaneh

Many of the families that left Yemen in 1881 and 1882 were very poor, so they had simple diets, and wheat was a big part of it. In the story, Saliman's family eats pita. Pita is flat and easy to stack. It would have been easy for them to make along the way.

But there are many types of Yemenite bread. Ayala's family also makes kubaneh, another traditional Jewish Yemenite bread. It was often baked on lower heat overnight and then eaten on Shabbat. Kubaneh is still eaten today by people from Yemen, as well as by many other people.

Please ask an adult for help before making this recipe, since it requires the use of an oven.

INGREDIENTS

2 cups all-purpose flour

4 tsp sugar

1 tsp instant yeast

1 ¼ tsp salt

¾ cup water

¼ to ½ cup butter
(softened at room temperature)

Directions

1) In a large bowl, mix together dry ingredients (flour, sugar, salt, and yeast). Add water to form a sticky dough.

2) Knead dough well until elastic and smooth.

3) Place dough in a bowl, and cover with a dish towel to rise at room temperature. Allow to double in volume (about 1 hour).

4) Punch dough and then divide into 4 even pieces and roll into balls.

5) Cover balls for about 15 minutes with a dish towel.

6) Flatten a ball and spread butter on each side. Then stretch as thin as possible with your hands. Don't worry about small tears in the dough.

Do-ahead tip: After step 3, you can cover the bowl tightly with plastic wrap and put it in the refrigerator for a few hours, until you're ready for the next step.

7) Once stretched, fold once into a thin rectangle, spreading more butter inside the fold.

8) Roll the rectangle into a cylinder shape (like a cinnamon roll). Lay flat and cut the roll in half.

9) Repeat for the 3 for remaining balls.

10) Generously grease a springform pan and place the rolls in, cut side up. They should be packed tightly in the middle of the pan (or use a small pan) so that they join together into a single loaf made up of individual rolls.

11) Cover and let rise again for about 45 minutes.

12) Preheat oven to 350 degrees.

13) Butter the top of the rolls.

14) Place the pan on a baking sheet and bake for about 30 minutes until golden brown. Pull apart into individual rolls.

Makes eight large rolls.